A Beginning-to-Read Book

It's a Good Game, Dear Dragon

by Margaret Hillert
Illustrated by David Schimmell

NORWOOD HOUSE PRESS

DEAR CAREGIVER,

The *Beginning-to-Read* series is a carefully written collection of classic readers you may remember from your own childhood. Each book features text comprised of common sight words to provide your child ample practice reading the words that appear most frequently in written text. The many additional details in the pictures enhance the story and offer the opportunity for you to help your child expand oral language and develop comprehension.

Begin by reading the story to your child, followed by letting him or her read familiar words and soon your child will be able to read the story independently. At each step of the way, be sure to praise your reader's efforts to build his or her confidence as an independent reader. Discuss the pictures and encourage your child to make connections between the story and his or her own life. At the end of the story, you will find reading activities and a word list that will help your child practice and strengthen beginning reading skills.

Above all, the most important part of the reading experience is to have fun and enjoy it!

Shannon Cannon

Shannon Cannon,
Literacy Consultant

Norwood House Press • P.O. Box 316598 • Chicago, Illinois 60631
For more information about Norwood House Press please visit our website at *www.norwoodhousepress.com* or call 866-565-2900.

Designer: The Design Lab

LIBRARY OF CONGRESS CATALOGING-IN-PUBLICATION DATA

Hillert, Margaret.
 It's a good game, dear dragon / Margaret Hillert ; illustrated by David Schimmell.
   p. cm. — (A beginning-to-read book)
   Summary: "A boy and his pet dragon play a game of soccer with friends and learn about sportsmanship"—Provided by publisher.
   ISBN-13: 978-1-59953-293-6 (library edition : alk. paper)
   ISBN-10: 1-59953-293-X (library edition : alk. paper) [1.
Dragons—Fiction. 2. Soccer—Fiction. 3. Sportsmanship—Fiction.] I.
Schimmell, David, ill. II. Title. III. Title: It is a good game, dear dragon.
   PZ7.H558In 2009
   [E]—dc22   2008037517

Manufactured in the United States of America.

Come on. Come on.
Run and get the ball.
We have to get to the game.

Yes, yes.
Here I am.
I have the ball.
We can go now.

You come, too.
I want you with me.
You can see what I do.
I play with this ball.
It is a good game.

Oh, look here.
Here it is.
This is the spot where
we play the game.

It is good to be here.
It is good to see you.
We are the blue ones.
You are red.
We will have fun.

We have to do this to put the ball in play.

Now, go, go, go.
Run, run, run.

And do THIS!

This way. This way.
Down this way.
We want to get the ball down there.

Now see this.
I will make it go in.

Oh, no.
It did not go in.

I can do THIS!

Oh, my.
You can do it, too.
You are a good help.

Here we go.
Run, run, run.
I will do it.

Look Out!
Look Out!

Oh, oh.
This is not good.
But we will get up
and play.

Look at them go.
Look at them go.
Oh, my. Oh, my.

Here we go, too.
Run, run, RUN-N-N!

Oh, no!
Now look at this.
Do you see this?

You are too good for us,
but we are good, too.
It was a good game.
We can be friends.
We can play and have fun.

Here you are with me.
And here I am with you.
Oh, what a good game, dear dragon.

READING REINFORCEMENT

The following activities support the findings of the National Reading Panel that determined the most effective components for reading instruction are: Phonemic Awareness, Phonics, Vocabulary, Fluency, and Text Comprehension.

Phonemic Awareness: Syllabication

Say the following words, clapping the syllables as you say them. Ask your child to tell you how many syllables are in each word:

play-1	ball-1	whistle-2	friend-1	soccer-2
happy-2	referee-3	winning-2	something-2	goalie-2
kick-1	breakfast-2	dragon-2	teammate-2	tipoff-2
children-2	trophy-2	mother-2		

Phonics: Syllabication

1. Write the following words on separate index cards:

soccer	little	running	jelly	supper
lesson	ladder	letter	silly	winning
happy	yellow	spotted	flipper	

2. Explain to your child that words that have two identical consonants in the middle are divided in between the two consonants.

3. Help your child cut each word in half between the double consonants.

Vocabulary: Movement Words

1. Write the following words on index cards and point to each card as you read the word to your child:

   run   kick   pass   toss   scores   block

2. Rearrange the cards and say each word in random order and ask your child to point to the correct word as you say it.

3. Rearrange the cards again and ask your child to read as many as he or she can.

4. Say the following sentences aloud and ask your child to point to the word that is described:

- When the ball goes into the net the team _____ a point. (scores)
- Soccer players have to _____ fast to keep up. (run)
- At the beginning of the match, the referee will _____ a coin in the air to see who goes first. (toss)
- The goalie's job is to _____ the ball from getting into the net. (block)
- Sometimes players need to _____ the ball to other players to move the ball down the field. (pass)
- In soccer, the players _____ the ball to move it down the field because they cannot carry it. (kick)

Fluency: Choral Reading

1. Reread the story with your child at least two more times while your child tracks the print by running a finger under the words as they are read. Ask your child to read the words he or she knows with you.

2. Reread the story aloud together. Be careful to read at a rate that your child can keep up with.

3. Repeat choral reading and allow your child to be the lead reader and ask him or her to change from a whisper to a loud voice while you follow along and change your voice.

Text Comprehension: Discussion Time

1. Ask your child to retell the sequence of events in the story.

2. To check comprehension, ask your child the following questions:
- Who is the adult wearing the whistle? What is his job?
- What is happening on page 9? Why does this happen at the beginning of a soccer match? How does it make the game fair?
- What is your favorite team sport to play or watch? Why?

It's a Good Game, Dear Dragon **uses the 65 words listed below.**
This list can be used to practice reading the words that appear in the text.
You may wish to write the words on index cards and use them to help your
child build automatic word recognition. Regular practice with these words
will enhance your child's fluency in reading connected text.

a	for	make	see	what
am	friends	me	spot	where
and	fun	my		will
are			the	with
at	game	no	them	
	get	not	there	yes
ball	go	now	this	you
be	good		to	
blue		oh	too	
but	have	on		
	help	ones	up	
can	here	out	us	
come				
	I	play	want	
dear	in	put	was	
did	is		way	
do	it	red	we	
down		run		
dragon	look			

ABOUT THE AUTHOR Margaret Hillert has written over 80 books for
children who are just learning to read. Her books
have been translated into many different languages and over a million children
throughout the world have read her books. She first started writing poetry as
a child and has continued to write for children and adults throughout her life. A
first grade teacher for 34 years, Margaret is now retired from teaching and lives in
Michigan where she likes to write, take walks in the morning, and care for her three cats.

Photograph by Glenna Washburn

ABOUT THE ADVISER Shannon Cannon contributed the activities pages that appear in
this book. Shannon serves as a literacy consultant and provides
staff development to help improve reading instruction. She is a frequent presenter at educational
conferences and workshops. Prior to this she worked as an elementary school teacher and as
president of a curriculum publishing company.